Cold Whispers

NIGHT of the GRAVEDIGGER

by Michael Teitelbaum

illustrated by Juan Manuel Moreno

BEARPORT
PUBLISHING

New York, New York

Credits

Cover, © Fer Gregory/Shutterstock and © Rob Byron/Shutterstock.

Publisher: Kenn Goin
Editorial Director: Natalie Lunis
Creative Director: Spencer Brinker
Text produced by Scout Books & Media Inc.

Library of Congress Cataloging-in-Publication Data in process at time of publication (2016)
Library of Congress Control Number: 2015013371
ISBN-13: 978-1-62724-805-1 (library binding)

For more information, write to Bearport Publishing Company, Inc., 45 West 21st Street, Suite 3B, New York, New York 10010. Printed in the United States of America.

10 9 8 7 6 5 4 3 2 1

Contents

CHAPTER 1

A Scary Dare

It was a week before Halloween. Jake Chestnut and his friends stood across the street from the old cemetery at the edge of his small California town. Jake had always been fascinated by the place. Many members of his own family had been buried there. But as far as he knew, no one had been buried in the cemetery for many years.

Jake's friends Ralphie, Pete, and Cheryl were also fascinated by the cemetery. They'd heard enough scary cemetery stories to be a little afraid of the place, too.

"So are we going to go into the cemetery after dark on Halloween or not?" asked Ralphie. At twelve, Ralphie was a year older than his three friends, and a real take-charge kind of guy.

"Sure, why not? What are we afraid of, right?" asked Cheryl, who had hung out with these guys since kindergarten. She felt good about never being afraid—or at least never letting anyone else know if she was.

"I guess there's nothing really to be scared of," added Pete, Jake's closest friend, who tended to be more of a follower than a leader. "What do you think, Jake?"

Before Jake could answer, a **gust** of wind slammed a sheet of newspaper against the back of his head. He shrieked.

"A little jumpy?" asked Ralphie. "I never knew anyone who was scared of newspapers. Don't be such a chicken."

"Come on, Jake," said Cheryl, teasing him. "Half the people buried in the Auburn Street Cemetery are your relatives. They should call the place 'The Chestnut Family Cemetery.'"

"It should be okay, Jake," added Pete. "Just think of our visit as a really strange family **reunion**."

"All right, I guess we can go," said Jake. "As long as we all go together. But you know what people say, right? The cemetery is haunted by ghosts of the dead. They also say strange figures wander around at night. And my favorite: No one entering the cemetery after dark will make it out alive!"

"Ah-oooohhh!" howled Cheryl, causing everyone to crack up.

"I snuck in there once after dark," said Ralphie, "and I made it out alive . . . or did I? YAAAAAAA!" Ralphie moved toward Jake, his arms outstretched, his face twisted, like a **zombie**.

"Nice, Ralphie," said Jake. "My heart almost popped out of my chest."

"So, are you in?" asked Cheryl. "I'm not scared."

"Well," said Jake. "If it's gotta be, it's gotta be."

"Wait," said Pete. "Are you saying that now, too? Your dad says it all the time."

"It's kind of a Chestnut family phrase," Jake explained. "Kind of like an old watch, passed down from generation to generation."

Ralphie leaned in close to Jake. "Maybe one of your relatives in the cemetery will rise from his grave, wrap his old, **rotted** hands around your throat and say, 'Well, if it's gotta be, it's gotta be!'" he said.

Jake just shook his head. "Funny, Ralphie. Real funny."

A week later, Halloween arrived. After dinner, at the time Jake usually went trick-or-treating, he headed out to meet his friends. Instead of dressing up in costumes, all four friends had decided to wear their soccer team jackets. Each one had the team's logo and the student's name. When they were all together in their matching jackets, they would look a bit like trick-or-treaters.

It was a dark night, and unusually chilly for October. Fog swirled through the streets that were filled with kids in costumes, adding to the overall Halloween feel.

A few minutes after leaving his house, Jake met his friends near the cemetery. The group walked quickly across the street, passing goblins, zombies, and witches, all hurrying along clutching their bags of goodies. The friends paused at the entrance to the cemetery—an old iron fence that towered high above the street. In the center of the fence was an opening where a rusty gate swung back and forth in the wind.

Squeeeeee!

"Wh-what was that?" Jake asked, looking all around.

"Cemetery monsters!" Ralphie said in a scary whisper.

"It's just a rusty old gate," said Pete. "Come on."

They stepped through the opening and into the cemetery. The sounds of trick-or-treaters faded with each step they took.

"The fog is even thicker in here than on the street," Jake said, feeling a chill in his bones. Nervous sweat broke out on his forehead.

Jake looked at several **headstones**, trying to push his fear aside, and focused on the family history carved into them.

"You can hardly see the headstones through the fog, guys," said Jake. "Guys?"

Jake looked around. There was no sign of his friends. He was standing in the cemetery, totally alone.

CHAPTER 2

The Man in the Cemetery

"Guys!" Jake shouted. "Pete! Ralphie! Cheryl!" No answer came, except for the echo of his own voice.

Jake stared into the dark night. The lights along the many paths winding throughout the cemetery cast an eerie glow through the fog. The cemetery seemed to stretch out forever in every direction.

Suddenly, the light Jake was under blinked, then went out completely. He was **plunged** into almost total darkness. Jake stumbled blindly, reaching his arms out before him. Suddenly, he felt something—*someone*—grab his shoulders.

"Get off!" Jake shouted as he struggled. He shoved the arms away from him, tumbling to the ground. The light blinked back on. Jake looked up at his attacker.

Shocked, he saw it was just a tree, its branches swinging in the wind.

10

Feeling foolish, Jake got back to his feet and continued along the path, hoping to find his friends. As he rounded a bend, a huge figure with wide wings stared down at him. He fell backward and gasped. Then he realized it was only a stone **monument** of an angel.

"This is nuts," Jake said to himself. "I'm leaving. I'll never find those guys in here."

He turned to head back in the direction he had come from. And that's when he saw something that made him shiver in fear.

Jake could just barely see a tall figure **shuffling** along through the cemetery, dragging something behind him that made a scraping, clanging sound. The man turned his head, and Jake could make out a pale face with hollow eyes.

The man spotted Jake and started walking toward him.

Jake turned and ran, his heart pounding, hoping he was headed in the right direction out of the cemetery. The fog closed in around him. He felt trapped. He glanced back over his shoulder every few steps to see if he was being followed. Because the fog was so thick, he couldn't tell—so he ran faster.

The legend is true! he thought. *Strange people do walk the cemetery at night.*

A few minutes later, the front gate came into view. Slowing down as he passed through the gate, he spotted his friends just outside the cemetery.

"What happened?" asked Pete. "We thought you were right there with us."

"Yeah, so did I," Jake said, gasping for air, his heart still pounding. "The place is so big and the fog is so thick, all I did was stop for a second and you were gone. But you won't believe what I saw."

"What? You met a few of your old relatives, and they invited you to join them?" joked Cheryl.

"I saw a really creepy-looking dude," Jake said. "He was tall and had long, stringy hair. His face was all wrinkly and his eyes looked almost like they weren't there."

"I know that guy!" said Ralphie dramatically.

All eyes turned toward him.

"I think he was my third grade teacher," Ralphie added.

"I'm serious," said Jake, realizing his friends didn't believe him. "I really saw this guy!"

13

"We have to find him," said Cheryl. "We have to go back into the cemetery and find this guy. We have to prove he's real."

"I believe you, Jake," said Pete. "I'll go back and look for this guy with you."

"You know you can count me in," said Ralphie. "Tomorrow night. We'll come back tomorrow night."

"You can tell your mom you're going to my house to work on a school project," Pete suggested. "We've worked on projects together before."

Jake's heart finally stopped pounding.

That's when a hand suddenly grabbed his shoulder. Fear shot through Jake's body like a **jolt** of electricity. He spun around and found himself face-to-face with a zombie.

"Trick or treat," the zombie growled through his rubber mask. "Hu-hu-huh!" The zombie laughed and then moved on.

Jake's friends all laughed. Jake did not.

"Don't worry so much," said Cheryl. "We'll be together when we go back tomorrow."

"All right," Jake said. "But next time, we all bring flashlights. I don't want to get trapped in the dark again in that place."

"Good idea," said Pete.

"Flashlights it is," agreed Cheryl.

"My dad has a 50-pound **generator** for when the power goes out," said Ralphie. "Do you want me to bring that, too?"

"Very funny, Ralphie," said Jake. "I'll see you guys tomorrow."

As he walked home, Jake tried his best to **convince** himself that it was going to be okay. *We'll all be together this time. And we'll have flashlights. And maybe my friends were right. Maybe I did imagine that guy. Maybe it was because I was so scared. Although, it sure felt like he was real!*

CHAPTER 3

A Very Bad Idea

The next night, Jake and his friends once again stood at the entrance to the cemetery. Jake had told his mother he was at Pete's house working on a school project. He felt bad about lying, although he *was* actually with Pete.

Jake stared through the iron fence and felt his heart start to beat faster. The noisy, crowded streets from the Halloween celebration the previous night were now silent and empty. The wind still whipped through the trees, though, and heavy fog still hung in the air.

And what about that strange man? Would they see him again tonight? And what would happen if they did?

"Flashlights on!" Cheryl said, taking charge. All four friends switched on their flashlights and stepped through the opening in the fence.

Jake immediately felt the hair on his neck rise. His heart started beating faster, even though nothing had happened. The eerie silence, combined with the thick fog, made Jake feel as if he'd been **transported** to another world. The four flashlight beams cut through the fog, casting strange shadows on the trees and headstones.

A low, sad moan broke the silence, sending chills through Jake's body. The others stood as still as stones.

"It's the man I saw last night!" cried Jake. "It has to be!"

A sudden loud flapping of wings came from above. Looking up, they saw a huge owl **emerge** from the fog, lifting up into the night sky.

"Never heard an owl before, Jake?" asked Ralphie, as the fog swirled around.

Jake shook his head, feeling foolish again. "Guess I'm a little bit jumpy," he said.

"A little?" said Cheryl.

"Okay, a lot," Jake admitted.

The group moved slowly through the silent cemetery, with Jake in the lead. The sound of Jake's footsteps crunching on fallen leaves sounded very loud to his ears. Dogs barked in the distance.

There was a sudden rustling in the leaves. Jake froze in his tracks and held his breath. He aimed his flashlight's beam toward the ground and saw . . . a squirrel running along the ground, kicking up leaves in its path.

Jake exhaled.

"Come on, Jake," said Pete, seeing how anxious his friend was. "It'll be okay."

Jake kept walking, picking up his pace. The sooner they made their way through the cemetery, the sooner he could leave.

"All right," he said, sweeping his flashlight beam across old headstones and trees. "I'm gonna get through this. After all, if it's gotta be, it's gotta be."

That's when his flashlight went dead.

"No!" he cried, flipping the switch on and off again and again. No luck. He stood still, trying to figure out what to do next.

"Guys!" Jake called out. Silence. "Oh no, not again. I guess they didn't see me make that last turn. How am I supposed to see where I'm going in all this fog without a flashlight?"

And that's when he heard the footsteps.

This time he was certain that it was no squirrel, no owl, no gust of wind. These were heavy footsteps walking though the leaves.

Jake backed away quickly . . . and crashed into a headstone. He stumbled again as he tried to find the path and the lights that could **illuminate** his way out.

When he finally came to a small pool of light, the man he had seen the night before was standing just a few feet away. Jake's feet felt as if they were glued to the ground. He couldn't move. And this time, Jake got a good look at the man.

The man had sunken eyes, and his skin was deathly white. He wore a long, torn coat. To Jake, it looked like dirt was falling in clumps from his ragged clothes. The man's scalp was peeling under his thin gray hair.

In his hands, the man clutched a shovel. He was standing beside a mound of freshly dug earth, next to a brand-new headstone.

The man looked Jake right in the eyes.

"Chestnut!" he growled in a thick **gravelly** voice.

Whose Grave Is This?

CHAPTER 4

Jake was stunned. A series of thoughts flashed through his mind:

The man is real. The man just dug a new grave in a cemetery where no one has been buried in years. THE MAN KNOWS MY NAME!!!

This last thought **propelled** Jake into action. He turned and ran as fast as he could, looking back over his shoulder. Before he could check where he was going, he crashed right into a body.

"Ahhh!" he screamed, tumbling to the ground, wondering if somehow the man with the shovel had managed to get in front of him.

Jake looked over and saw Ralphie lying in the dirt.

"What happened to you?" Ralphie asked as he and Jake got back to their feet. Cheryl and Pete stood beside them.

"Where did you go?"

"I saw him again," Jake said **frantically**, ignoring the question. "He had just dug a fresh grave . . . and . . . and he said my name."

"He said your name?" Pete asked.

"He said 'Chestnut,'" Jake replied. "How could he know my name?"

"Um," Ralphie said, pointing at Jake's jacket, "maybe he read it!"

Jake looked down at the name on his team jacket and sighed in relief.

"I think we need to go back again," said Cheryl.

"Are you crazy!" Jake said, shaking his head.

"We've got to get home now. It's getting late. But we'll *all* go back," replied Pete. "Together. We gotta find this guy!"

23

That night, when he got home, Jake's mother was sitting at the kitchen table.

"Hi, honey, how's the project with Pete going?" she asked as Jake joined her at the table.

"Okay," was all Jake replied. Then, after a short pause, he said, "So I walked past the old cemetery on the way home from Pete's. I kinda peeked in. No one gets buried there any more, right?" he asked.

"Oh, yeah, no one has been buried there in years," Jake's mom said. "In fact, your grandfather was the last person buried in that cemetery."

Jake had never met his grandfather, though he was named after him.

"What was he like?" Jake asked.

"Grandpa? He was a very successful lawyer," explained Jake's mom as she showed Jake a picture of his grandfather. "He had a great life . . . until he learned that he had sent an innocent man to jail for a crime he didn't commit. Unfortunately, he didn't discover that until after the innocent man had died in prison. Your grandfather spent the rest of his life filled with guilt."

"Wow," said Jake. "How terrible for Grandpa . . . and for that poor innocent man."

As Jake headed to his room to do some homework, he thought about returning to the cemetery the next night with his friends. He was scared, but he was also curious. As his mother said, no one had been buried in that cemetery for decades. So what was that man doing there with a shovel, beside a freshly dug grave?

Jake and his friends once again gathered at the entrance to the cemetery the following night.

"I must be crazy for going back in there," said Jake, pulling a new flashlight out of his jacket pocket.

"Don't worry, we'll be there with you, Jake," said Pete, who felt bad about getting separated from Jake the previous two nights.

The fog was even thicker than it had been the two nights before. But all four friends kept their flashlights lit and focused in front of them. And Jake made an extra point of keeping his friends in sight.

As he slowly made his way through the cemetery, Jake shined his flashlight on the headstones. Almost every one was the grave of a member of the Chestnut family.

The group paused at the grave of Jacob Henry Chestnut.

"Who's that?" asked Cheryl. "He has your name."

"That's my grandfather," Jake explained. "In fact, I was named for him."

Suddenly, Jake heard a rustling sound nearby. "Who's there?" he cried, pushing aside a branch and shining his flashlight into the bushes.

Nothing.

Shifting the light to the left a bit, the beam revealed a freshly dug, empty grave—the grave Jake had seen the night before.

"How can there be a new grave?" asked Ralphie.

"I told you," said Jake. "I saw this last night. And I saw the guy who dug it."

Jake shined his flashlight up to the headstone and froze in terror.

"Jacob Henry Chestnut, Jr.," read Cheryl, staring wide-eyed at Jake. "That's you!"

"I-I don't understand," **stammered** Jake.

R.I.P

JACOB HENRY
CHESTNUT, JR.

"Chestnut!" boomed a voice from the dark.

Jake turned around and found himself face-to-face with the gravedigger.

"Chestnut! Your grandfather sent me to jail for a crime I did not commit," **snarled** the gravedigger. "Now you will pay!"

The gravedigger lifted the shovel over his head. Jake took a step back and tumbled into the open grave.

"I died in jail, an innocent man. But my spirit cannot rest in peace until I have **avenged** the wrong done to me," shouted the gravedigger. He tossed a shovelful of dirt onto Jake.

"Leave me alone!" Jake screamed, frantically brushing the dirt from his hair.

Another scoop of dirt landed on his head.

"Get me out of here!" Jake yelled.

"My life was ruined," growled the gravedigger, tossing more dirt onto Jake.

"I'm sorry for what happened," Jake yelled. "It was a mistake!"

The gravedigger paused for a second, but then he made a growling sound.

"Guys, help!" cried Jake. He tried to claw his way out of the grave, but he kept slipping.

Cheryl, Pete, and Ralphie reached down and pulled Jake up. Then they all stepped back slowly.

The gravedigger took a step towards them, shaking the shovel at Jake. "I'll get you, Chestnut!" he roared.

There wasn't time to think. "Run!" Jake shouted.

As they ran for the exit, Jake looked back. The gravedigger roared, "If you ever come back here, Chestnut, I'll be waiting for you!"

"Let's go home," Ralphie said, panting to catch his breath as the friends reached the sidewalk.

"We're with you on that," said Cheryl. Pete, wide-eyed, nodded in agreement.

Jake knew one thing for sure: he would never ever set foot in the cemetery again! Never!

The Night of the Gravedigger

1. Why were Jake and his friends fascinated with the cemetery? Give examples from the story.

2. Would you agree to go back to the cemetery after you saw the mysterious gravedigger? Why or why not?

3. What does Jake learn about his grandfather in this scene?

4. What did the gravedigger want from Jake? Use examples from the story to explain.

5. What has Jake just discovered in the cemetery in this picture?

6. A legend is a story from the past that cannot be proven to be true. In the story, Jake mentions the legend of the cemetery—that strange people walk there at night. Can you think of a legend about where you live?

GLOSSARY

avenged (uh-VENJD) got even with someone who harmed you

convince (kuhn-VINS) to make someone believe something

emerge (i-MURJ) to come out from somewhere hidden

frantically (FRAN-tik-lee) nervously

generator (JEN-uh-*ray*-tur) a machine that creates electricity

gravelly (GRAV-uhl-ee) rough sounding

gust (GUHST) a sudden rush of wind

headstones (HED-*stohnz*) stones used to mark the locations of graves

illuminate (ih-LOO-muh-*nate*) to light something up

jolt (JOHLT) a sudden burst

monument (MAHN-yuh-muhnt) a statue built to remember a person or event

plunged (PLUHNJD) fell quickly and steeply

propelled (pru-PEHLD) pushed or motivated

reunion (ree-YOON-yuhn) a gathering of people who haven't seen each other for a long time

rotted (RAH-tid) decayed, falling apart

shuffling (SHUHF-uhl-ing) walking slowly, dragging the feet along the ground or floor

snarled (SNARLD) said in a threatening way

stammered (STAM-uhrd) spoke with many pauses or repetitions

transported (trans-POR-tid) moved from one place to another

zombie (ZAHM-bee) a dead person who appears to be alive

ABOUT THE AUTHOR

Michael Teitelbaum is the author of more than 150 children's books, including young adult and middle-grade novels, tie-in novelizations, and picture books. His most recent books are *The Very Hungry Zombie: A Parody* and its sequel *The Very Thirsty Vampire: A Parody,* both created with illustrator Jon Apple. Michael and his wife, Sheleigah, live with two talkative cats in a farmhouse (as yet unhaunted) in upstate New York.

ABOUT THE ILLUSTRATOR

Juan Manuel Moreno was born in Buenos Aires, Argentina, and he has always loved drawing. His art is noted for its range of styles and techniques. In 2003, Juan and his wife, Patricia, decided to travel throughout South and North America, and they lived in several different countries. In 2006, they crossed the Atlantic Ocean and settled in Barcelona, Spain. Juan, his wife, and their two daughters, Nina and Tessa, now split their time living in both Spain and Argentina.